TO: EUAN

To: 老劉

Chapman

For my parents, for having filled my childhood
with wonderful trips and colored pencils.

Marina García

She was born in Buenos Aires, Argentina, on an
Autumn morning of the last century. Since she was a
child she loved to wander around telling her stories
and drawing everywhere.
When she grew up she became an architect, which
she loved a lot as well; but not too long ago she left
the world of building to dedicate herself to write and
illustrate books for children because she loves doing
this much more than the other.
It all began some years ago, when she arrived in
Spain to visit her grandparents and, as if by magic,
she never left the country again...
Today, she lives in Seville with her little son Nicolás,
and she has published several travelling
and art books for children.

Mateo at the Museum
A trip to the Thyssen

Text and illustrations

Marina García

SerreS

Original title: Mateo de paseo por...El Museo Thyssen

Translation: Cambridge University Press, Barcelona

Text and illustrations
© 2002 Marina García Gurevich
lucanor@teleline.es

© 2002 Ediciones Serres, S. L.
Muntaner, 391 – 08021 – Barcelona

English rights for all speaking countries

First Edition, 2002

ISBN: 84-8488-069-9

Editorial Design: Estudio Marina García

Printed in Spain by Sagrafic, S. L.
D.L.: B – 34.474 - 2002

¡¡Rriingg!! That afternoon, my grandma's voice on the telephone seemed very mysterious.

"Mateo, get ready. I'm taking you out on a very special trip".

"Where to, Grandma?" I asked, thinking at the least we would go to the cinema or a new circus with clowns, elephants and wild tigers.

Grandma always took me to the most exciting places!

"Ah! ...I'm taking you to a surprise place," she said. And, without saying more, she hung up. It made me wonder, intrigued..."Where would Grandma take me this time?"

"Where would Grandma take me this time?"

I got on Lightning, my red hobby-horse, brave as the horses in westerns, and I waited for grandma very impatiently.

But when she arrived with all her painting tools, I imagined the worst:

GRANDMA HAD OTHER PLANS!

"We're going to the Thyssen-Bornemisza. It's a museum you'll really like" she said as she came in. "You'll see..."

I didn't like this at all. Lightning and I followed her, heads down, while tigers and lions went "pop!" in my head and vanished into thin air...

A MUSEUM!?...Bah! I'd forgotten my grandma likes painting so much and
goes to museums to copy her favourite pictures.
"Pictures tell us lots of things..." she said.
"...They tell us about landscapes and real cities and places imagined by
painters. They tell us what people used to be like, what they did
or how the artist imagined them to be..."

"...Ah! I nearly forgot: you like horses,
tigers and lions, don't you? Well, let's see..."

When we were inside the museum we crossed an enormous room and, a little further on, Grandma stopped in front of a picture where a woman was hugging an enormous cockerel. Underneath, it said something like: "The Cock" Marc Chagall, 1928.
"Why is she hugging the cockerel, Grandma?" I asked, while I watched how she got her paints ready.
"I think they love each other a lot," she answered. "Chagall liked to paint his feelings. He did that by listening freely to his heart. Do you like it?"
-Pssssh...LIKE IT? The truth is I was getting sleepy...

...very sleepy!

The Cock
Marc Chagall, 1928

Then I saw it...
"Hello Mateo. My name's Blue!" said the little horse, who, naturally, was blue. "I live in a picture in this museum and now I must be getting back."
"And how did you get out?" I asked, very curiously.

"The pictures have a secret entrance so you can walk around inside or get out for a walk like me," said Blue.
"Do you want to come with me?"

Walking around **inside** pictures?...

yin a flash we made **a great leap...**

The horse was saying surprising things. Without thinking twice, I held on to him like the woman did to the cockerel. And...

Oh!...

We went through a window with *broken glass!*
Luckily it turned out it wasn't a window and didn't have broken glass. That
was just as well: if I'd done that much damage, I'd be in trouble.
"It's just a window painted in the picture. If you look carefully, you can *see*
that part of the landscape has fallen out as well as the glass" explained Blue.
"And it's our way in to THE IMAGINARY WORLD!"

The Key to the Field
René Magritte, 1936

One...

Two...

Three!

*Madonna of Humility with
Angels and a Donor*
Anonymous Venetian, c.1360

As many as six golden angels came out to meet us!
"Heaven is golden like our heavenly wings," they sang
in chorus. "Would you like to come with us?"
Blue didn't give me time to answer...
Off he went trotting off behind a Knight riding to
his castle.

Chuut!

We approached the castle silently so we wouldn't frighten the birds and animals. They seemed very peaceful. But a brown dog discovered us and growled. I tried to calm it down: "shhhh!"
A white stoat heard me. It got very scared and ran off.
Then, the knight in shining armour began to draw his sword and...
We had to hide among the flowers!

*Young Knight
in a Landscape*
Vittore Carpaccio, 1510

Flowers...and more flowers...Flowers that looked like **smudges**...Or were they smudges smelling of **flowers?**

Whatever they were, I really wanted **to plunge into** them and play with them...

"Watch it! Don't tread on my flowers!" someone cried very angrily.

"If you get close, you will see little smudges. But if you move away, they turn into flowers: a whole garden painted by me!" added the proud voice.
"Right, now clear off!"
"It's Renoir. He likes painting the sunlight outdoors," whispered Blue. And off we went, slowly and quietly...

*Woman with Parasol
in a Garden*
Pierre-Auguste Renoir, 1873

The girl with the white parasol,
next to the gardener, waved us goodbye.

A very beautiful tune coming from the end of the garden... From among those flowers?... Or was it **something else?**

A girl, hidden behind something, seemed to want to tell us something...

"They aren't flowers. If you look carefully, you'll see they are ballerinas' skirts" explained the girl in the orange costume. "Can you see them dancing on stage?" "I can only see one," I said. "Ahhh!, but there's another leg and part of another costume!" "Do you want to dance with us?" asked the nicest one, beckoning with her hand. We went round and round together. Then we left through a little door behind the stage...

Goodbye pretty girls!

Tilted Ballerina
Edgar Degas, c.1877-1879

Crreeaakk!...

The door squeaked when Blue pushed it with his muzzle.
"Everything is a bit dark here," I warned, a bit scared.
"And I think they're spying on us..."

"**Who** are you?" someone interrupted in an unfriendly voice.

"**What** are you doing here?" added another.

"**Mmmmm...** they look very handsome!" said the sweetest voice.

"**Ha! Ha!**...What fun! A boy with a blue horse!"

Haaalttt!

"Do you know who I am?" said a man with a serious face – a very serious face.
"I am Henry VIII, the most powerful king in the world! Look at my splendid
clothes and finest jewels. Admire me. That's what I'm here for!"
"Noo!" shouted someone with a clown's voice. "Look at me, just me!
My name is Harlequin and when I'm not looking at myself in the mirror, I
dance and sing and do lots of fun tricks."

*Portrait of Henry VIII of
England*
Hans Holbein the Younger, c.1534-36

Harlequin with Mirror
Pablo Picasso, 1923

Ha! Ha! What a bunch of show-offs and bigheads!

Merzbild 1st
(*The Psychiatrist*)
Kurt Schwitters, 1919

What was all that? Bits of canvas, cardboard,
wire, a coin and even a cigarette!
"It's a collage," explained Blue.
"Merzbild is always laughing because he finds
everything funny."
"He looks very strange with that
bobbin-shaped ear!" I said, surprised.
"Well, let's hope we find out what is filling this
up with smoke," he added.
"This IS very strange!"

OOHH!
The smoke was coming out of a strange puzzle made out of colour cutouts.
"What is this?" I exclaimed, shocked.
"It's my friend the smoker," replied Blue, enjoying himself. "If you look carefully,
you can see his nose, ear, eye, his shirt collar and even his cigar!
It was very difficult to see him through so much smoke, but it looked like his
hat had opened up like a fan.

The Smoker
Juan Gris, 1913

When the smoke began to vanish, coloured balloons appeared...
Lots of blue and red balloons filled the room.

Glop...glop

Glop...glop

"Mateo, do you want to play?" asked Blue, nudging the balloons with his muzzle.

Glu...glu

¡"What fun! They're like soap bubbles. Where can they all be coming from?"

Glop...glop

Woman in the Bath
Roy Lichtenstein, 1963

"Of course I like you!" I said, half in love.
I also liked her. She was beautiful, a bit like comic-book
drawings, but I didn't say so.
I ran after Blue so I wouldn't lose sight of him...

"Listen, Blue, aren't there any streets in your world?"
I asked, following behind.
"Streets?" Blue laughed and neighed loudly. "There are whole cities!
Would you like to find them?"
"Great!" I said, without really meaning it. "Cities inside a museum?"
"Well, follow me and you'll see how lovely and different they are," said
Blue and, without further ado, he began to trot between the coloured
ribbons in an unknown direction...

¿¡!??

"But what's this?"
In front of me were lots of coloured ribbons crisscrossing each other everywhere.
"It's Mondrian's imaginary city!" shouted Blue. "The ribbons are its streets and the
squares its parks and houses. It's as if you were looking down from the sky!"
"Yeah, it's true!" Blue was always surprising me, he knew so much.
Pity we can't see a railway station from the air, I like them so much...

New York City, New York
Piet Mondrian, 1940-42

Chooo!... Chooo!

"Would you like to see some trains?" asked Blue. "There's one coming out of that red tunnel. It'll stop right in front of that yellow signal."

"Wow! That's just like my wooden train station" I said, amazed at the similarity.

"You know, Blue, sometimes we pick up my grandma from the station and there are always lots of people there. But here there's nobody...

Where can they be?

The Large Railway Picture
László Moholy-Nagy, 1920

Oouuuch!...

Just as I was thinking this, a large crowd nearly flattened me.
They were running from one side to the other and shouting.
The streetlamps lit up the streets and I could see everything quite red"
Let's go, Mateo!" shouted Blue, and we ran out of the city. I don't Know if it
was real or imaginary but the people were very noisy.
It reminded me of Gran Via at Christmas!

Metropolis
George Grosz, 1916-17

Splish!... Splash!... Splosh!

Is it starting to rain or... is it
my imagination?
"It seems very real." answered Blue.
"The floor is all shining wet and you can
even hear the wheels of the vehicles."
"Come on, Blue. Let's splash about a bit
in the puddles!" I laughed, while
the colours melted around my feet.
Mr Pisarro, who was spying at us
through the window while he was
painting, thought it was having lots of
fun seeing us play in his rainy city.

*Rue de Saint Honoré in the
Afternoon. Rain Effect*
Camille Pissarro, 1897

¡Ha! Ha! What fun this is!

Ha! Ha! This is fantastic!

The laughs came from a park and a huge tree filtering the sunlight.
"We're having a picnic!" said a girl, laughing, as she leaned on a branch. "What do you think of the seesaw we made?"

The Seesaw
Jean-Honoré Fragonard, 1750-52

"Seesaw? "Where?"
"Can't you *see* it here, underneath?" said the girl. "It's made from a plank, a tree trunk and a stone. It turned out *brilliant*!

¡Sssshhh!

"Don't shout so much! I can't rest! The roaring of wild beasts and my neighbour's snores are quite enough, thankyou."

Grrr!...Grrr!

Grrr!

"The voice is coming from the wood," said Blue and there he trotted off.

There, next to the waterfall, a maiden was resting peacefully.

"Hellooo!" she said, stretching, "I'm the goddess of Love, but everyone calls me Venus."

"Would you lend me your bow and arrows?" I asked excitedly.

"No way!" she replied. "They are my friend Cupid's and he might get very angry."

"Pity!" I said. "I wanted to shoot at those ferocious tigers and that long-legged elephant!"

"Don't worry, they're harmless!" said the maiden, stretching.

"They are just in my dreams. And, with that, she went back to sleep.

The most annoying thing was the buzzing of that bee going round and round!

Nynph of the Spring
Lucas Cranach, El Viejo, 1530-34

Dream caused by the Flight of a Bee around a Pomegranate a Second before to wake up
Salvador Dalí, 1944

Bzzz... Bzzz...

It seemed like the buzzing was following us...
But it turned out to be lots of butterflies. Hundreds of them fluttering around
the path, which had become wavy and shining. It made us want to run, play
and tumble down! Which is what we did...
"You know, Mateo? These colours remind me of my house," said Blue.
And his eyes sparkled with happiness.
"We must be near by now!"

we tumbled down...

We played,

and we ran back and forth!

Waterloo Bridge
André Derain, 1906

The butterflies had turned into a
bridge, a river with boats and
a gigantic sun.
You just had to step back to see!

Then a yellow field appeared,
waving in the wind, and a sky as
blue as my friend.
"There at the end you can see a
house with a red roof!"
he exclaimed very happily.
"Is that your house?"
But Blue shook his head and
kept trotting...

"Les Vessenots " en Auvers
Vincent Van Gogh, 1890

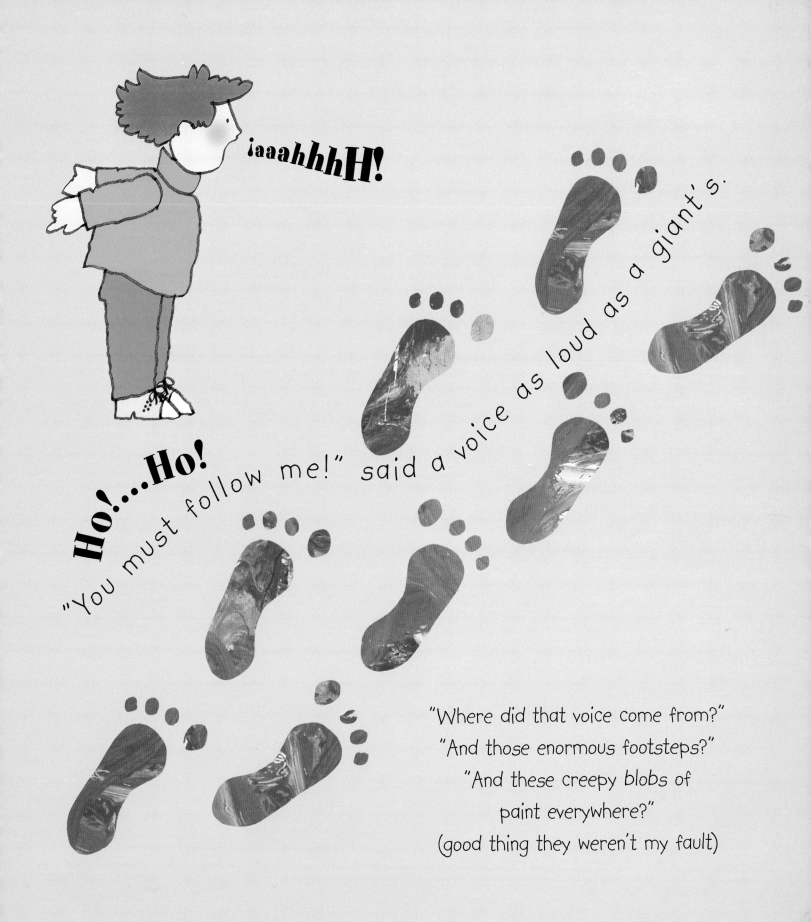

Ha!...Ha!

"Don't be frightened," the voice went on,
which actually was a giant's.
"I also like walking in the museum."
"Oh!"...It was very hard to see him pro-
perly with so much paint. He looked
like he'd been painted with fingers!
"Look how his moustache moves!" said
Blue, killing himself with laughter.
The red man waved, his
hand dripping paint. Then he popped
back into his picture.
"Doesn't he remind you of Father
Christmas, all dressed in red?" I asked,
but Blue didn't seem to be listening...

"Blue?...Where are you?

Red Man with Moustache
Willem de Kooning, 1971

"MATEOOOO!!!" Can you hear me?!!" my grandma's voice gave me a terrible fright. "Look what a lovely painting! A young girl with a lion, a yellow house and red and blue horses." "B L U E !!!" I exclaimed with surprise when I saw my friend in there. "Have you ever seen a blue horse?" asked Grandma.

The Dream
Franz Marc, 1912

¿¡!?

It looked like Blue was flapping his ears and dying of laughter.
Then I winked at him so he knew I could keep
a secret, and answered:
"Really? Really? NEVER!! Only in my dreams, Grandma..."
My grandma knows a lot about painting but definitely nothing
about blue horses going on walks round museums.

How could I explain that to her?

"ONLY IN MY DREAMS!!" I shouted again, very happily.
And I left with Lightning, galloping home behind her.

With M for Mateo

We left the Thyssen-Bornemisza Museum and went for a walk. We waved at the horses at the fountain of Neptune, and Grandma showed me a huge museum she promised to take me to another day: the Prado Museum.

Then we entered the Retiro Park. There were lots of people walking around like us. I wanted to go for a boat ride on the lake, but my grandma said no. She was scared...

But right after she gave me an enormous balloon and a strawberry ice cream just how I like them...and we went home as happy as could be.

¡Mmmm!...

At home, I decided to make a collage to tell everyone about my fantastic trip through the museum and so I wouldn't forget anything I had seen.
I glued things I liked onto my pad of paper. Then I did some small drawings to show what I liked most. Why don't you make a collage too?

Why don't you make a collage too?

With M for Museum..

12

1

5

9

10

2

11

3

4

6

7

8

1. *The Cook,* Marc Chagall (1928)/ 2.*The Key to the Field,* René Magritte (1936)/ 3. *Madonna of Humility with Angels and a Donor,* Anónimo veneciano (c. 1360)/ 4. *Young Knigth in a Landscape,* Vittore Carpaccio (1510)/

5. *Woman with Parasol in a Garden,* Pierre-Auguste Renoir (1873)/ 6. *Tilted Ballerina,* Edgar Degas (c.1877-1879)/

7. *Portrait of Henry VIII of England,* Hans Holbein -El joven (c.1534-1536)/ 8. *Harlequin with Mirror,* Pablo Picasso (1923)/ 9. *Merzbild 1ˢᵗ (The Psychiatrist),* Kurt Schwitters (1919)/

10. *The Smoker,* Juan Gris (1913)/ 11. *Woman in the Bath,* Roy Lichtenstein (1963)/

12. *New York City, New York,* Piet Mondrian (1940-1942)

Here are all the paintings in Mateo and Blue's adventure
which are in the Thyssen-Bornemisza Museum.
You can get an idea of their actual size by comparing them to the size of the visitors.
Did you think they would be so big or small?
Try and find them in each of the rooms of the museum.

13. **The Large Railway Picture,** László Moholy-Nagy (1920)/ 14.**Metropolis,** George Groz (1916-1917)/ 15. **Rue de Saint Honoré in the Afternoon. Rain effect,** Camille Pissarro (1897)/

16. **The Seesaw,** Jean-Honoré Fragonard (1750-1755)/

17. **Nymph of the Spring,** Lucas Cranach -El Viejo (1530-1534)/ 18. **Dream caused by the Flight of a Bee around a Pomegranate a Second before to wake up,** Salvador Dalí (1944)/ 19. **Waterloo Bridge,** André Derain (1906)/ 20. **"Les vessenots" en Auvers,** Vincent Van Gogh (1890)/

21. **Red Man with Moustache,** Willem de Kooning (1971)/ 22. **The Dream,** Franz Marc (1912)

Photographic Aknowledgments © Fundación Colección Thyssen-Bornemisza, Madrid, 2002